This igloo book belongs to:

....

Contents

Cinderella .... page 4

Rapunzel .... page 12

Sleeping Beauty .... page 20

The Emperor's New Clothes .... page 28

Thumbelina .... page 36

The Princess and the Pea .... page 44

igloobooks

Published in 2016
by Igloo Books Ltd
Cottage Farm
Sywell
NN6 0BJ
www.igloobooks.com

LEO002 0616
10 9 8 7 6 5 4 3 2
ISBN: 978-1-78440-175-7

Illustrated by Diane Le Feyer

Printed and manufactured in China

My 6-in-1 Treasury
Cinderella
and other
Fairytales

igloobooks

Cinderella

Once, a girl lived with her cruel stepmother and mean stepsisters. They were jealous of her and made her dress in rags and sweep cinders from the grate. "We shall call you Cinderella," they said, laughing wickedly.

One day, an invitation to a royal ball arrived. "We shall all go," said the stepmother. "All except you, Cinderella. Your clothes are far too dirty and besides, you must help us to get ready."

So, Cinderella helped her wicked stepmother and her mean stepsisters get ready for the ball.

Soon, the stepmother and stepsisters left for the ball. "I wish I could go, too," said Cinderella with a sob. Suddenly, a beautiful fairy appeared. "I'm your fairy godmother," she said and she waved her wand.

PING! A pumpkin turned into a golden coach, four mice into white horses and two rats into fine, elegant footmen. ZING! Cinderella's ragged dress changed into a beautiful ballgown and dainty glass slippers appeared on her feet.

"Remember to leave the ball before midnight," said the fairy godmother. "That's when the magic ends."

At the ball, Cinderella met the handsome prince. He instantly fell in love with her and they danced and danced to the beautiful music.

Then, the clock struck midnight. "I must go," cried
Cinderella and she dashed down the stairs and out
of the palace. The prince ran after Cinderella, but
she had gone. All he found was a single, delicate glass
slipper lying on the steps.

The prince searched the kingdom for Cinderella.
"I will marry the girl whose foot fits in this slipper,"
he declared. The stepsisters tried the dainty slipper,
but they couldn't make it fit. When Cinderella tried,
the slipper fitted perfectly.

The prince asked Cinderella to marry him.
They had a beautiful wedding and never saw the
stepmother, or stepsisters ever again. After that,
Cinderella and her prince lived happily ever after.

Rapunzel

Long ago, lived a man whose wife was expecting a child. The wife wanted some rapunzel flowers and the only place they grew was in a witch's garden. So, one day the man crept in to pick some.

Suddenly, the furious witch appeared. "If you take that, you must give me your child when it is born!" she shrieked. The man was so frightened of the witch, he agreed.

A week later, a baby girl was born. The witch took her and named her Rapunzel.

Rapunzel grew to be a beautiful, young woman.
The witch kept her in a tower and each day she called
out, "Rapunzel, Rapunzel, let down your hair."

Rapunzel dangled her long, golden
hair out of the window and the
witch climbed up it.

One day, a handsome prince saw the witch climb up Rapunzel's hair. When the witch had gone, the prince called out, "Rapunzel, Rapunzel, let down your hair."

So, Rapunzel hung her hair out of the window and the prince climbed up.

Rapunzel and the prince fell in love and he visited her every day. However, the clever witch found out and she was so angry, she snipped off Rapunzel's hair, then banished her to the depths of the forest.

"Rapunzel, Rapunzel, let down your hair," called the prince, the next day. When the prince climbed up, however, he found the witch. "Aargh!" he cried, letting go and falling to the ground below.

The prince searched the woods for days and days, but could not find Rapunzel. "I will never find her," he said, sadly and began to weep. Just then, he heard someone singing. Sitting by a stream was Rapunzel.

The prince was overjoyed to see Rapunzel. "I shall take you to my kingdom," said the prince, "and make you my wife." So, the prince took Rapunzel back to his royal castle. They were never troubled by the witch again and lived happily ever after.

Sleeping Beauty

Long ago, a king and queen celebrated the birth of their daughter. Three fairies came to give the princess magical gifts. One gave kindness, another beauty.

The third fairy was about to give her gift when a bad fairy burst in. "You dare to forget me!" she screeched. "My gift is that on her sixteenth birthday, your daughter will prick her finger on a spindle and die." With that, the bad fairy disappeared.

"The princess won't die," said the third fairy. "She will sleep for a hundred years."

Years passed and the curse was forgotten. Then, on
her sixteenth birthday, the princess was wandering in
the castle when she found a secret door. It led to
a room where an old woman was busy spinning.

"Come closer, my dear," said the old woman with a smile. The princess reached forward to touch the spindle, but suddenly pricked her finger. "Ouch," she said, slumping onto a bed and falling into a deep sleep.

At that same moment, the whole palace fell under
the spell of sleep.

Months and years passed by and a thick tangle of
thorns grew everywhere. Stories of the sleeping beauty
in the hidden palace spread far and wide.

One day, a handsome prince came riding by. "This must be the enchanted palace," he said. "I must find the sleeping beauty." The prince sliced through the brambles until he reached the inner courtyard of the palace.

When the prince found the sleeping princess, his heart filled with love. He kissed her gently on her cheek and Sleeping Beauty opened her beautiful eyes. She looked at the prince and fell instantly in love.

Everyone else in the palace woke up, too and there was great joy and celebration. The king and queen were very happy. At last, the bad fairy's spell had been broken and they could all live happily ever after.

The Emperor's New Clothes

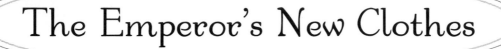

There was once an emperor who loved clothes so much that he had a wardrobe the size of a house. The problem was that no matter how many fine and beautiful things the emperor bought, he always wanted more.

One day, two swindlers, who planned to trick the emperor, came to the palace. "We make outfits from cloth so fine, stupid people cannot see it," they said. "I must have one," said the emperor and he gave the swindlers a bag of gold.

The swindlers sat at empty looms. They convinced the emperor's minister that they were weaving the finest cloth ever seen and that only stupid people could not see it. The minister did not want to seem stupid, so he agreed.

When the emperor heard that his minister had seen the cloth, he was very excited. He summoned the swindlers to his throne room and insisted that they hurry and finish his new outfit. "It is already done, Emperor," said the swindlers.

The emperor ran to the sewing room where he saw the empty looms. "If I'm not clever enough to see the cloth, everyone will think I'm too stupid to be ruler," he whispered. So, the emperor pretended that he could see the new outfit.

The swindlers pretended to dress the emperor in the new clothes. He paraded in front of the mirror and admired his reflection. "I shall have a royal parade to show them off," announced the emperor.

So, the emperor set off wearing nothing but a headdress and a pair of white pants.

The crowd didn't want to seem stupid, so they clapped and cheered. Then, a small boy shouted, "He looks naked!" The boy laughed and laughed.

Soon, everyone else was laughing. At first, the emperor was annoyed. Then, he realised he had been cleverly tricked. "How foolish I have been," he said, laughing. "Now I have learned my lesson." Everyone agreed that it was a good thing and they never forgot the story of the emperor's new clothes.

Thumbelina

Long ago, a woman found a tiny girl in her magic flower garden. "She's smaller than my thumb," said the woman, "so I'll call her Thumbelina." She lay Thumbelina in a walnut shell and took her home.

One day, a toad took Thumbelina. "You can marry my son," she said, putting the girl on a lily pad. Thumbelina was just wondering how she could escape when a fish nibbled through the stem and the lily pad floated away.

As she drifted downstream, a butterfly fluttered past and Thumbelina tied it to the ribbon of her dress. It pulled the lily pad even faster down the river, until a big beetle swooped down and carried her away.

The beetle flew Thumbelina to where his family
lived, but they just laughed at her. "What a funny
looking thing," they said. "Please take it away."
So, the beetle flew into the woods and dropped
Thumbelina on a daisy.

Thumbelina stayed in the woods until winter came. It was very cold, so she took shelter in a cosy house where a mouse lived. Thumbelina was very happy and even made friends with a swallow who had an injured wing.

One day, as the swallow prepared to fly away,
a grumpy old mole came to visit Mouse at his house.
"I wish to marry Thumbelina," he said. "I shall take
her beneath the earth to my underground home."

Thumbelina began to cry. She looked up at the
lovely, blue sky. "I don't want to live in the dark with
a horrid, old mole," she sobbed.

Suddenly, her friend the swallow swooped down,
swept her onto his back and flew far away.

The swallow flew to a wild flower meadow, where
Thumbelina saw a little man wearing a crown.
"I'm the flower king," he said. "Will you be my queen?"
"Yes!" said Thumbelina, who was happy at last to
have found her true home.

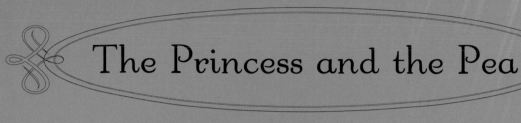

The Princess and the Pea

Once, there lived a prince who wanted a wife who was a true princess. He travelled all over the world, but could not find one. In despair, the prince returned home to the castle where the king and queen lived.

Then, one stormy night, there was a knock at the palace door. "I am a princess," said a wet and bedraggled girl. "I lost my way in the storm." The king took pity on the girl and asked her to stay.

"I will see if she is a real princess," said the queen to the king. She told the servants to put a pea on a bed and pile twenty mattresses on top. "Bedtime," she said to the girl, "sleep well."

The girl did not sleep well. "There was a hard lump in the bed," she complained, the next morning.

The queen smiled at the king. "Only a true princess would feel a tiny pea through all those mattresses," she said.

The king and queen introduced the princess to the prince and they fell instantly in love.

There was a wonderful royal wedding and the little, green pea was put in a glass case so that everyone could see it.